THE INVINCIBLE
IRON MAN™

WITHDRAWN

AN ORIGIN STORY

Based on the Marvel comic book series **The Invincible Iron Man**

Adapted by Rich Thomas

Interior Illustrated by Craig Rousseau *and* Hi-Fi Design

New York

www.marvel.com

TM & © 2011 Marvel & Subs.

Published by Marvel Press, an imprint of Disney Book Group. No part of this book may be reproduced or transmitted in any form or by any means, electronic or mechanical, including photocopying, recording, or by any information storage and retrieval system, without written permission from the publisher. For information address Marvel Press, 114 Fifth Avenue, New York, New York 10011-5690.

Jacket and Case Illustrated by Pat Olliffe and Brian Miller
Designed by Jason Wojtowicz

Printed in the United States of America
First Edition
1 3 5 7 9 10 8 6 4 2
G942-9090-6-11227
ISBN 978-1-4231-4287-4

This is **TONY STARK.**

Tony is usually as regular a guy as you or me
—but with **a lot more money.**

When Tony puts on his special armor, he becomes more **powerful** than most people.

He even calls himself something different—

THE INVINCIBLE IRON MAN!

But Tony wasn't born a Super Hero.

He hasn't always fought
to **protect** people.

But with **villains on the loose**, such as **Titanium Man**
and **Iron Monger**—who both use Tony's technology for their
own evil purposes—

Tony feels it's his responsibility to stop them!

Tony didn't always get the job done this easily.

Or this well.

A while ago, Tony's armor **wasn't so sleek.**

In fact, when he first became Iron Man,
Tony's armor **didn't even shine!**

But if you really want to know how Iron Man was born, we need to start with the **man behind the mask.**

We need to start with Tony.

Tony had so much money that he could go anywhere he wanted.

He loved to **have fun.**

And he loved the **finer things** in life.

But Tony also worked hard. He was
a **brilliant inventor.** He knew
all sorts of things about **science.**

He loved to work with **magnetic fields**.
Using them, he a created a powerful energy
force that he called **repulsor technology**.

The military was interested in Tony's work. In fact, it was in a **secret Army lab** that Tony's life was forever changed.

An enemy Army had attacked, and Tony was **badly hurt!**

Since Tony was famous, he was recognized right away.

The enemy knew all about his inventions.

They tossed him in a **prison room** filled with electronic and mechanical equipment. They wanted him to create a mighty weapon for them.

To make things worse, before the enemy left the tiny cell, they told Tony that **his heart had been hurt** in the blast. He did not have much longer to live.

Tony soon found he was not alone in the cell.

The enemy had captured another famous scientist—
PROFESSOR YINSEN.

The enemy wanted the two men to
work together on the great weapon.

The two men **worked tirelessly** to create

something that would save Tony's life. . . .

Finally, they **completed the device** that Tony would always need to wear on his chest to keep his heart beating.

But that wasn't **all** they created.

Tony put on the armor . . .

. . . and proved that no walls could hold
the IRON MAN!

It didn't take long for

the enemy to realize . . .

... they were fighting
a losing battle.

Having **escaped from prison** and saved
Professor Yinsen, Tony flew back home.

But almost as soon as he got there, he realized
that he could now **help** where others couldn't.

Tony to the rescue!

He was strong, unstoppable, FRIGHTENING!

Maybe a little **too** frightening.

Tony had an **idea.**

There.
That was better.

Almost better.

Back to the **drawing board.**

Tony thought that Iron Man needed something as **smooth and stylish** as Tony was.

He needed to create **a lighter suit.**

All he needed was for **his chest plate to remain attached** so his heart would not stop beating.

Everything else could be **changed.**

And a new **Iron Man** was born!

As Iron Man, Tony never stops **protecting** people all over the world.

And when he's not fighting for justice as **Iron Man**…

. . . Tony runs his company,
Stark Industries.

Stark Industries might need
Tony to be **a businessman,**

but with new villains attacking every
day, the world needs Tony to be

an **Iron Man!**